THE NEW AGE

FLAYMAR
THE SCORCHED
BLAZE

With special thanks to Michael Ford

To Zane Wentzell, one of the zaniest people alive!

www.beastquest.co.uk

ORCHARD BOOKS
338 Euston Road, London NW1 3BH
Orchard Books Australia
Level 17/207 Kent St, Sydney, NSW 2000

A Paperback Original
First published in Great Britain in 2012

Beast Quest is a registered trademark of Beast Quest Limited
Series created by Beast Quest Limited, London

Text © Beast Quest Limited 2012
Inside illustrations by Pulsar Estudio (Beehive Illustration)
Cover by Steve Sims © Beast Quest Limited 2012

A CIP catalogue record for this book is available from
the British Library.

ISBN 978 1 40831 844 7

5 7 9 10 8 6

Printed and bound by CPI Group (UK) Ltd, Croydon, CR0 4YY

The paper and board used in this paperback are natural recyclable
products made from wood grown in sustainable forests. The
manufacturing processes conform to the environmental regulations of
the country of origin.

Orchard Books is a division of Hachette Children's Books,
an Hachette UK company

www.hachette.co.uk

FLAYMAR
THE SCORCHED
BLAZE

BY ADAM BLADE

ORCHARD

THE SEA-CLIFF

THE
PLAINS

DESERT

VELORA

KENSA'S
CASTLE

Henkrall

FORESTED SINKHOLE

GREAT NORTHERN MARKET

GEYSER ISLAND

I heard of Avantia in my youth, when I flew with the other children over the plains of Henkrall. They said it was a land of beauty, bravery and honour. A place of noble Beasts, too.

Even then it made me sick.

I can't fly now. My cruel mistress, Kensa, was jealous of my wings, so she took them. Don't pity me, Avantians – it's you who should be afraid. Your time is coming. Kensa has plans for your green and pleasant land. Your Good Beasts will be no defence against her servants – they'll be powerless!

You'll need more than courage to protect you from the Beasts of Henkrall!

Your sworn enemy,

Igor

PROLOGUE

Nema soared above the volcanic landscape with its black rocks and pools of green, sulphurous water. He checked back over his shoulder and saw his friend, Aber, gaining on him.

Nema lifted his left wing a fraction. His feathers caught an updraft and sent him veering down and to the right.

"Catch me if you can!" he shouted. Aber was the stronger flyer, but Nema was more agile. That's why their games of tag were so evenly matched.

Nema swooped low over the island, and spotted tell-tale bubbles on the surface of a pool. He dodged as a surge of water shot from the ground in a mighty column, then fell back in a cascade of steaming spray. They didn't call this place Geyser Island for nothing. The lava that surrounded the island in a huge lake also flowed beneath it, heating the water to boiling point and sending it spouting into the sky like fountains.

Nema slalomed between the shooting geysers, keeping his eyes peeled. He'd never been caught in one yet – he was too quick – but he'd had lots of close calls. There was nothing like the feeling of the warm spray on his face and feathers.

He glanced round. No sign of Aber. *Lost him!* thought Nema.

A shadow fell over his back. Too late! Aber swooped down and tapped Nema's shoulder with his foot. He hovered above Nema, grinning.

"You're it!" he said, then flew off.

Nema climbed after his friend.

Aber was quick in a straight line, but the geysers in the middle of the island sprouted densely. Nema made quick changes of direction to avoid them, and gained on Aber. As his friend twisted to miss one geyser, another caught him under his wing. Nema saw Aber spin, limbs flailing, and swooped in quickly. He wrapped his arms around Aber's chest and guided him to the ground. The rock was warm beneath Nema's feet.

"Thanks!" said Aber. "I thought that was going to be a crash-landing!"

"Maybe we should be getting back,"

said Nema. "If my parents find out we've crossed the lava lake again, we'll be grounded for days."

"My grandpa wouldn't even notice if I flew in on golden wings," said Aber. "But you're right – let's go."

They took off and flew back towards the shoreline. Their village, on the mainland of Henkrall, was just a dark smudge through the heat-haze over the lava lake. Aber and Nema glided on the hot air, out of reach of the shooting geysers, through clouds of shifting vapour.

"Is your grandpa still spending all his time in the workshop?" asked Nema.

"Every day," Aber replied. "He was supposed to have retired, but now he's up before dawn and back after sunset."

"What's he doing in there?"

"No one knows," said Aber. "He

won't let anyone inside, but the other day I managed to sneak a look."

Nema turned to his friend. "And?"

"Well…" Aber began. His words turned to a scream as something black rose from below.

It took Nema a moment to realise it was a hand – a giant hand with fingers that snatched Aber around his middle, crushing his wings against his body. He was dragged back through the steam with a shriek of pain.

"Aber!" Nema called, dipping his wings and plunging after his friend.

Aber lay on the ground, one wing dangling useless and broken at his side, the other scorched with a red-raw burn. He wasn't moving. But that wasn't what chilled Nema's blood in his veins. Behind his friend towered a huge creature. The heat of its body made Nema's eyes run with tears. He could see its limbs were burning coals, black in the centre, white hot at the edges. A cloak of pure flickering flame brushed the rock at its feet, and bright red locks of fire hung from its head.

"Tell Jaffrey his time is running out," the Beast hissed, her voice like the crackle of spitting logs and falling ash.

"Who…?" Nema said. "What are you?"

The Beast's black face split into a jagged smile. "An old friend of Jaffrey's," she said. "Tell him if he wants to see his grandson again, he will fulfil his promise."

Nema looked to his injured friend. Though his eyes were closed, his chest was moving up and down. He was alive. But there was no way Nema could reach him. He managed to find strength in his wings to take off.

The fire-clad Beast watched
him with blazing eyes as he flew
back towards the village. He didn't
understand what the message meant.
All he could do was deliver it. What
was Aber's grandfather up to in that
workshop? Would anyone believe
what had happened on Geyser Island?

And would he ever see Aber alive again?

15

CHAPTER ONE

DANGER TO THE SOUTH

"Let's land!" said Tom. He gently
pushed at the base of Tempest's
purple mane. The flying stallion
dipped through the air towards
a craggy rock. With barely a jolt,
his hooves met the ground and he
cantered to a stop, folding his mighty
wings to his side. Elenna swooped
down on Spark. The wolf hovered for

a moment, then closed his wings mid-air and dropped onto his four paws.

"I still can't get used to it," she said, as she climbed off the wolf's shaggy back.

"Do you think anyone will believe it when we get back to Avantia? That all the creatures of Henkrall can fly?"

Tom smiled at his friend, but inside he was deadly serious.

If we get back, he thought.

They'd travelled to this strange kingdom by a forbidden form of magic called the Lightning Path. Tom remembered the feeling – searing hot and freezing cold at the same time – as the lightning had struck the enchanted staff he was holding. One moment they'd been standing on King Hugo's battlements, the next they were here.

Even Aduro had counselled against using the magic at first, though he'd finally given in. There was no other way they could face their latest enemy, Kensa the Witch. She'd summoned the Lightning Path to enter Avantia and steal the blood of the six Good Beasts. Using her magic, she'd mixed the blood with six figurines made from Henkrall's earth and created six new Beasts. Any of them would be powerful enough to destroy Henkrall, and Tom had sworn to defeat them all. So far, he had succeeded, but three remained.

Using the powerful sight gifted to him by the Golden Helmet, he could see in the distance a band of people heading through the sky towards the centre of the kingdom. Like every person and animal here, they had the gift of flight. The men and women were setting off from the village Tom and Elenna had just left. They were going to face Kensa. *They're brave,* he thought. *I hope they succeed.*

Tom checked his shield-map to see where the next Beast awaited them. When they'd first arrived here, carried on a fork of lightning, the six tokens had vanished from his shield, breaking his contact with the six Good Beasts of Avantia. In their place, a map had appeared, showing the alien kingdom of Henkrall and guiding him towards each new threat. Every time Tom defeated a Beast, its heart turned into one of the tokens. Sepron's fang, Epos's talon and Nanook's bell were back where they belonged.

A golden line glowed from the wooden surface, leading towards the south of the kingdom, and a name was etched in the shield – it read *Flaymar*.

"It looks like another Beast is

waiting for us," said Elenna.

They took off once more, flying south. Tom missed Storm desperately, and he knew Elenna felt the same about Silver, but their new animals had so far proved themselves brave and loyal during the Quest.

They'll need all their spirit to face three more Beasts, Tom thought.

They swept over the vast central plains of Henkrall. Tom marvelled at a flying herd of cattle, settling beneath them on a grassy slope. The soft draft of Tempest's wings was hypnotic, but Tom forced himself to concentrate, adjusting their course to take them towards Kensa's next Beast. At her workshop, Tom had heard Kensa's ultimate plan – to bring her Beasts to Avantia. He wasn't sure how she intended to do it, but he couldn't let even one of her creations into his home kingdom.

"Tom!" called Elenna, breaking into his thoughts. "What's that?"

His friend was pointing ahead, and Tom stared. His heart thumped as he saw the shape of a giant torso in the distance, looming amid a group of buildings. A huge head on square shoulders seemed to gaze right at them.

"It must be Flaymar," Tom shouted, letting his hand rest on the hilt of his sword.

The Beast watched them approach without moving. Tom urged Tempest on, ready to fight. If Flaymar was among the buildings of a town already, there was no telling what damage it might be causing.

But as they came closer, doubt crept into Tom's mind. *Why isn't the Beast moving? Why isn't it getting ready for an attack?*

Flaymar's massive head was covered

in grey skin, like ancient stone.
Tom and Elenna flew over the low
buildings of the town. The Beast sat
in a central square, its arms hanging
by its sides, resting on a plinth. Tom
saw the Beast's skin wasn't grey like
stone – it *was* stone. Its broad features
were carved smooth, its eyes just
hollows. This was no Beast.

"It's a statue!" he said.

CHAPTER TWO

WARRIOR OF STONE

They swooped past the figure. Tom had faced several Beasts made of stone before, but this one was completely lifeless.

"You're right!" called Elenna.

Patches of weeds and moss covered the statue's weathered surface, and here and there stone flaked away. It looked ancient. If this wasn't a Beast, what was it a statue of?

As he wheeled over the town for another pass, Tom saw an orange haze beyond, glowing like the lava of Stonewin's crater in Avantia. *Perhaps they have volcanoes here too*, Tom thought. But this looked more like a vast sea. Checking his shield, he saw the route to the next Beast led that way. *With a name like Flaymar, that makes sense.*

The town had houses and barns, with smoke rising from chimneys. Like many of Henkrall's buildings, there were doors in the roofs, or halfway up walls, for the flying folk to take off and land. But Tom couldn't see any people.

Elenna flew alongside him. "Perhaps we should buy some food for the animals," she said. "It might be the last opportunity we get for a while."

Part of Tom wanted to press on
towards the fiery horizon, but he
knew Elenna was right. Without their
animals being at full strength, this
Quest would be impossible. Plus, Tom
was curious about the statue. Who
had built such a thing, and what
was it for?

"Let's go and take a look," he said.

They dropped into the central
square, landing their animals in
front of the statue. After Tom had
dismounted, Tempest flexed his
wings and whinnied. Spark barked
nervously, and Tom saw a shape
moving between two buildings.
It looked like a boy. He called out
"Wait!" but whoever it was vanished.

"Where is everyone?" asked Elenna.

Tom shrugged. He walked up to
the base of the statue, running his

hand over the cold stone. Each of
the figure's huge feet was as big as
a cart. The rough stone was covered
in discoloured patches and bird
droppings.

"It's like some sort of totem," Tom
said in wonder, letting his eyes travel
up the solid body. About halfway up,
over the Beast's chest, a dull glint
caught his eyes. "What's that?" he
muttered, pointing.

Elenna squinted. "Some sort of
marble plaque," she said. "I think
it has writing on it."

Backing away, he used the power of
the Golden Helmet to see the details.
He focused his vision on the panel.
It was about as tall as he was and
marked with the shape of a hand.
Beneath it four lines of script were
carved.

He read them aloud:

"Blood of hero, flesh and bone,
Wake the ancient heart of stone.
In the time of direst need,
Save the town with bravest deed."

"It sounds like some sort of prophecy," said Elenna.

"Or an old legend," said Tom.

The sound of a footstep made them spin around.

Five winged folk stood there – three men and two women. *They must have landed silently*, Tom thought. Each held a weapon – two swords, a threshing flail, a spear and an axe.

"Who do you think you are?" asked the man in the centre.

Tom considered drawing his sword, and knew Elenna would be ready

with her bow in the blink of an eye.
But could they face five foes at once?

"We're not your enemies," he said,
raising his hands.

"Then what are you doing sneaking
around the Great Protector?"

So that's the statue's name, Tom
thought.

"We're not sneaking anywhere,"

said Elenna. "We came to buy food for our animals."

"She might be telling the truth, Prentas," said the woman with the axe.

The man's eyes narrowed. He raised the tip of his spear towards Tom's neck. "I don't trust them," he said. "Where are their wings?"

Tom stared levelly at him, trying to ignore the deadly point at his throat. "We're not from this kingdom, Prentas," he said. "We've come to fight a common enemy." He pointed towards where he'd seen the lava on the horizon. "A Beast of fire."

The townsfolk looked to each other, muttering under their breaths and shaking their heads. All but two lowered their weapons.

"You're coming to Jaffrey," said

Prentas, gesturing with his spear. "He'll know what to do with you."

Tom was sure now that he could take these townsfolk on if he had to. *They're scared*, he thought. *They know something about Flaymar they're not letting on. Whoever this Jaffrey was, it sounded as if he was in charge. He might be able to help us.*

"We'll come peacefully," said Tom, "but please feed our animals."

Prentas shot a look among his companions, who all nodded. "Very well," he grumbled. "Take them to a stable, Vilma."

As Tom and Elenna followed the leader one way, a woman sheathed her sword and led Tempest by the reins in the other direction. Spark looked to Elenna.

"Go on," she said. The wolf yawned

wide and followed the woman too.

Prentas led them past a low barn with no windows. They passed two sets of double doors in the side, both padlocked with thick chains. Tom heard a grinding sound from within, followed by ringing blows like a blacksmith's forge.

"What's in there?" Elenna asked.

"None of your business," said Prentas. "It's Jaffrey's workshop."

At the end of the barn, a ramshackle shed had been built with a leaning roof. Prentas knocked at the door with three hard raps of his spear butt. The banging sound inside stopped, and Tom heard the shuffling of feet and heavy bolts being drawn back. The door opened a crack. "What now?" grumbled a voice.

"Strangers," said Prentas. "Snooping

around the Great Protector."

The door opened further, and Tom saw an old man's bristled, lined face. "Strangers, eh? In Herrinfell? Well, I'm busy. Leave me alone!"

As the door began to close again,

Tom broke his silence.

"Please, Jaffrey," he said. "Tell us what's going on."

The elderly man paused. "Nothing's going on. We don't like snoopers round here. Get rid of them, Prentas."

Tom shoved his foot in the door. "We're not snoopers," he said. "We have a common enemy – Kensa."

At the sound of the name, blood rushed to Jaffrey's face. "Get rid of them, Prentas," he said.

With that, the door slammed shut.

CHAPTER THREE

HERRINFELL'S SECRET

Tom felt a sword point in his back.

"That's enough," said the woman with the axe. "Jaffrey's had his say, and you're to clear off from Herrinfell."

"Take your animals and be in the sky at once," said Prentas.

"What's going on here?" asked Tom. "What's the big secret about Kensa?"

The woman hefted the axe above her shoulder. "I'd go now, if I were you," she said. "Or you won't be going at all."

Tom stared at the scowling faces of the townsfolk. *They're not going to talk*, he thought, *and we've got a Quest to fulfil.*

"We'll go," he said, "but you're making a mistake."

He let himself be ushered back to the square, where Tempest and Spark were waiting, looking refreshed. The stallion neighed to see Tom again and dragged his fore-hoof eagerly across the ground. Tom climbed onto the flying horse and Elenna mounted Spark.

"We won't be as nice if we see your faces again," said Prentas.

Tom fought back the urge to reply.

Why are we being treated like this? He squeezed Tempest's flanks and the horse galloped and spread his wings. They took off over the square.

"What a strange town," Elenna said.

"They're hiding something," said Tom, "but we'll never know what it is. We have to head further south."

They steered their animals and flew over the buildings of the town. As they reached the outskirts, something caught Tom's eye. A boy was flying low through a street below, waving up at them. *The boy from the shadows,* Tom thought. *He wants us to land.*

He whistled to Elenna and pointed downward. She saw the boy too and nodded.

Together they descended and landed silently in a deserted alleyway.

The boy approached them cautiously.

"It's all right," whispered Elenna.
"We're friends."

The boy's face broke into a weak
smile. "You're the only hope against
that...that thing," he said. Tom could
see fear behind his eyes.

"Tell me what happened," he said.

"My name is Nema," said the boy. He pointed south, his finger trembling. "Yesterday, Aber and I were playing over Geyser Island when something attacked us." Tears rose to his eyes. "She took my friend."

"She?" said Elenna.

"A monster," Nema said. "A creature made of flaming boulders. She must have come from the lava lake."

A Beast, thought Tom. *Flaymar*.

"And do the other people of Herrinfell know about it?" he asked.

Nema nodded. "Aber is Jaffrey's nephew. He's got some sort of deal with her. He's making something in his workshop."

Tom frowned. "What?"

Nema shook his head, tears welling in his eyes. "I don't know. Jaffrey used to be a metalworker – the best in the kingdom. But he stopped work years ago. Please, help my friend, Aber. He's stuck on the island with that horrible creature."

Elenna hugged the sobbing boy, and Tom stared back into the town. He was torn. We should be flying straight to the island to face the Beast, but...

"What should we do?" asked Elenna.

Tom made up his mind. "That workshop holds answers," he said. "We need to get inside."

"You can't," said Nema, wiping his eyes. "It's locked up."

Tom raised his eyebrows. "A few locks never stopped us. Can you guard our animals?"

Nema nodded. "Be careful."

Tom and Elenna crept back through the streets on foot, stopping to peer around corners, and shrinking back into the shadows whenever they heard a sound. Tom used the looming figure of the Great Protector to guide them. Soon they reached the workshop and sneaked along the side until they reached a set of locked doors. Tom drew his sword and raised it over the padlock.

"This might be noisy," he whispered.

"Wait!" said Elenna, raising her hand. "Use the jewel in your belt instead."

"Good thinking!" said Tom, sheathing his sword.

He took the purple jewel from his

belt and held it beside the lock. A fine beam of indigo light struck the lock, heating it red, then white hot. Smoke trailed from the metal as the beam cut through it. The padlock dropped with a thunk to the ground and Tom pushed open the door.

Gloom shrouded the interior of the workshop. Tom peered inside, looking for any sign of movement. There was no one about. Through cracks in the timber walls, shafts of light illuminated dancing motes of dust in the air.

"It's safe," he muttered. "Jaffrey must still be in his shed at the far end." He stepped through the door and Elenna followed close behind.

The old beams of a barn roof arched overhead, but this was no barn. Lumps of metal littered the ground, and a huge hearth at the far end glowed with flame. Something rested on a long stone table and stand in the centre of the chamber. Whatever the object was, it was twenty paces long and covered with a filthy sheet.

Tom gripped a corner, took a deep breath and pulled the sheet away.

Elenna gasped. "It can't be!"

Tom recognised what he was seeing at once. "A Lightning Staff," he said.

Resting on the stands was a huge metal rod, glinting in the semi-darkness. Its surface was etched from top to tail in strange markings – ridges and swirls and stars and letters of an ancient language. It was identical to the one they'd used to travel from Avantia to Henkrall, which Tom had let go of and lost.

Identical except for the size – this

was ten times as large as theirs!

"No person could lift that," said Elenna.

Tom sensed the horrible power of the object before him.

"It's not designed for a person,"
he said, his skin cold. "It's meant for
a Beast. Kensa's Beast. We have to
stop her."

"I'm afraid you won't get the
chance," growled a voice.

Tom and Elenna jerked around.
Jaffrey stood by another door,
holding a device that looked like
a giant mechanical crossbow. Two
bolts were loaded.

Then the old man pulled the
trigger.

CHAPTER FOUR

KENSA'S BLACKMAIL

Tom shoved Elenna out of the way and raised his shield. A double thud almost knocked him off his feet.

As Jaffrey cursed and struggled to reload, Elenna placed an arrow to her bowstring and levelled it at the old man. "That's enough," she said. "Drop your weapon."

"Do as she says," Tom warned.

The old man let the crossbow fall

from his hands. "Please don't hurt me," he begged. "I had no choice."

Tom pulled the shafts from his shield and threw them to the ground. He looked up at the staff. "You made this for Kensa, didn't you?" he asked.

Jaffrey nodded and sank to his knees. Elenna lowered her bow.

Tom approached the old man, but didn't draw his sword. "Tell us what happened," he said. "Why are

you working with an evil witch like Kensa?"

Jaffrey looked at Tom with watery eyes. Now that they were closer, Tom could see he had many feathers missing from his wings, and those that were left were sparse and grey. He doubted whether Jaffrey could fly at all.

"I used to know Kensa, years ago," said the old man, "when she first arrived in Henkrall."

"When she was banished here," said Elenna.

"We invented things together in her mountain workshop," said Jaffrey. "With her clever designs, and my metalwork skills, we could have been quite a team…"

"But something happened?" said Tom.

"I opened my eyes," said Jaffrey, shaking his head. "I saw the evil that lay behind her plans, and I swore I'd have nothing more to do with her. I came home to Herrinfell to be with my family."

"Kensa's Beast has your grandson," said Elenna.

Jaffrey's eyes widened in surprise. "How do you know that?"

"Never mind," said Tom, staring hard at him. "You must have been making this staff long before she kidnapped Aber."

"Ah, but I didn't know it was for Kensa then," said Jaffrey. "A strange one-eyed hunchback visited me."

"Igor!" Tom and Elenna said together.

"Yes," said Jaffrey. "Poor fellow, I thought, because somehow he'd lost his wings. He brought a plan, a detailed drawing of this staff. I told him I'd retired years ago, but he offered me so much money, I would have been a fool to say no."

"And you had no idea who it was for?" said Tom. He was growing impatient. He had a Quest to fulfil!

"Not until two days ago," said Jaffrey. "Igor came back on his flying hog. He told me Kensa was growing impatient. Well, when I heard she was behind it, I refused to carry on."

"And let me guess," said Tom. "Kensa didn't like that?"

"I offered to give back all the money... I offered to give back more, but the hunchback wouldn't take no for an answer. That's when they took Aber. The staff is almost finished now – it's my only hope of seeing my grandson again."

Tom stroked the strange markings, imagining a Beast clutching the staff. A Beast of Henkrall let loose in Avantia could cause countless deaths, especially if he and Elenna were stuck here, unable to get home.

"Kensa must not have this," he said.

Jaffrey shook his head. "But—"

"We will get Aber back," Tom said. "Then the hold that witch has over you will be broken. Understand?"

"It's you who needs to understand," said Jaffrey, climbing to his feet. "Kensa is too powerful. You don't stand a chance."

Tom summoned the courage from the golden breastplate, feeling it swell in his chest. "We've had a taste of her power," he said. "But while there's blood in my veins, I won't let Kensa prevail."

The quick patter of footsteps sounded outside and Nema ran into the workshop.

"What are you doing here?" asked Jaffrey.

"Quick!" said the boy to Tom. "Prentas and the others spotted your animals. They know you're still here!"

Tom drew his sword. "I'll explain – they'll be reasonable."

"No," said Jaffrey, gripping his arm. "Prentas has a temper unlike any other in Herrinfell. They'll let their weapons do the talking."

They heard more pounding feet heading along the alley outside, then Prentas's shout. "Surround the place. Block all doors!"

Jaffrey pointed to the far end of the workshop, where a ladder led up to a hatch in the wall. "That will take you to the roof – it's the only way."

"He's right," said Elenna. "We should run – the Quest is more important."

Tom nodded and they headed towards the ladder, climbing quickly. As Elenna opened the hatch and went through, an arrow lodged in the wall beside Tom's head. He didn't look back and followed his friend onto the gently sloping tiled roof.

"Where are they?" shouted a voice.

"Not this way!" Tom heard another call.

"They're on the roof!" cried Prentas. "Kill them!"

"They'll find," hissed Tom. "Let's go!"

He and Elenna ran, sending loose roof-tiles scattering and smashing below. Prentas, airborne, appeared to one side. "I warned you!" he shouted, lifting his spear.

A flying woman with a bow rose up at the other side of the barn. "You should have stayed away!" she said.

Tom heard a neighing ahead. He

gripped Elenna's hand and tugged
her after him towards the end of
the roof. He saw the man with the
axe swooping towards them. At any
moment Tom expected to feel a blade
in his back.

Tom and Elenna sprinted on.
"There's nowhere to go!" she shouted.

"Trust me!" said Tom.

Then he leapt off the edge, pulling
a screaming Elenna with him.

CHAPTER FIVE

FLAYMAR'S LAIR

They landed with a thump across Tempest's back. The stallion dipped a little in the air, then rose steadily with powerful wing strokes. Elenna slipped off and landed on Spark's shaggy pelt. "That was close!" she said, as the wolf carried her higher.

Tom righted himself, swinging a leg over Tempest's strong flank to straddle his back.

"We're not clear yet!" he said.

Tom heard the flap of wings and glanced back. Prentas was closing the gap between them, lunging with his spear. Tom managed to duck and draw his sword. As the angry attacker stabbed again, Tom brought his blade down onto the spear shaft, severing it. The point tumbled through the air.

Prentas backed away, drawing a dagger from a strap around his ankle. He waved to the other townsfolk. "After them!"

Tom urged Tempest on and Elenna did the same with Spark. For a while their angry pursuers kept pace, but soon they slowed and gave up the chase.

"Don't come back!" Prentas bellowed.

"They really don't like strangers," said Elenna.

"I don't think they wanted to follow us this way," said Tom. He patted Tempest's neck. "We owe these two a big thank you."

Elenna ruffled her hand in Spark's fur. "We certainly do."

They pressed on south, and soon they reached the shores of a huge

lake of rippling lava. Tempest, so
brave in the town, started tossing his
head. Currents of hot air and wisps of
smoke rose between them, and Tom
flew higher, pulling his tunic over his
nose and mouth. At first, the island
ahead looked black as jet, with ridges
and cliffs and craters pockmarking
the landscape. As they came closer
Tom saw pools of pale water dotted
around the barren ground. Occasional
fountains of water spouted, then fell
to earth in steaming clouds. A few
hardy grasses and shrubs sprouted
from between the rocks, and the
charred stumps of old trees reached
like gnarled, stubby fingers. There
were puddles of bubbling lava too.

"Geyser Island," said Elenna.

It's a dead land, Tom thought.
The perfect home for a Beast.

He scanned the ground, looking for any sign of life. Elenna drifted towards him.

"Aber could be anywhere," she said.

"If he's still alive," said Tom. "Perhaps we should split up to search."

Elenna looked unsure, then a smile broke over her lips. "I know!" she said. "We could use Spark's nose to sniff him out."

Tom nodded. "If he's half as good as Silver, that might work."

Elenna leaned close to Spark's ears and muttered to him. She pointed to her nose and to the island. The wolf must have understood, because he immediately dropped closer down. He glided across the landscape with just the occasional wingbeat, ears back and nose twitching. Tom followed not far behind.

Spark veered left and right, back
and forth, then suddenly flew in a
straight line at speed.

"He's found something!" Elenna
called back.

They zipped over several pools of
water, down a narrow gorge and
through the falling geyser fountain,
then Tom saw a shape on the ground
– a boy.

"Aber!" Tom called. "Hold on – we'll be with you soon."

The boy looked up, and started waving frantically. Tom could see one of his wings was broken and useless, while the other flapped weakly. Tom passed overhead, but there was no sign of any Beast. He and Elenna wheeled around to land. The geysers were close together here, and the air felt wet and warm like a jungle.

Tom slowed as he passed over a pool of lava and Tempest landed smoothly a few paces from the boy.

"Who are you?" asked Aber, his eyes darting around nervously. Elenna landed as well.

"My name is Tom," he replied. "And this is Elenna. Jaffrey sent us to rescue you. We must be quick – we've heard there's a Beast—"

"Look out!" Aber cried.

Tom felt heat at his back and he staggered, shielding Aber with his body. The pool of lava nearby was spitting and bubbling wildly. Something black and massive rose from its centre. It seemed like a boulder, or a giant ember from the fire – solid and deadly. More rocks followed, stacked and pressed together in the shape of a body.

The creature stepped from the molten pool, scattering droplets of fire. Two blazing eyes stared at them, and a cloak of flame trailed over the ground. Familiar symbols danced across its surface. Tom couldn't deny what he was seeing. The Beast had red hair, long locks of fire. The shape of the body was like someone Tom knew well, even if it was in a Beast's form.

"Kensa!" Elenna gasped.

"Not quite," rasped the Witch's voice. "Meet the Beast I've created in my own image – Flaymar, the Scorching Blaze."

CHAPTER SIX

PROTECTOR OF HENKRALL

Tom drew his sword and pointed it at the Beast's chest.

"We know your plan," he said. "We've seen the staff you plan to use to send a Beast to Avantia."

Flaymar laughed. "Then you know your kingdom is doomed."

"Not while we can fight on," said Tom. He pushed Aber towards

Elenna. "Get him to safety. I'll handle Kensa's Beast."

He leapt towards the Scorching Blaze, squinting at the tremendous heat, and hacked at the Beast's leg. She roared and seemed to crumple like a falling turret. Tom leapt back to avoid being burnt as Flaymar's whole body collapsed in a shower of ash and sparks. All that was left was a pool of lava and shattered stone.

Can it be that easy? Tom wondered.

The lava spilled into a crack in the ground and vanished.

"She'll be back," Aber shouted. "We need to get away now before—"

His words were drowned by the sizzle of fire leaping from the ground behind him. Flaymar's body reassembled like a tower of stacked coals right above Elenna and Spark, limbs aflame. She lifted a foot, massive as a burning haycart, ready to crush them.

Tom didn't think. With a roar of defiance, he ran at the Beast's other leg, shield first. Heat baked his face and fire licked over the shield's edge as he slammed into the Beast. Flaymar wobbled, and her foot crashed down beside Elenna, who seized Aber and dragged him onto Spark's back. "Fly!" she cried to the wolf.

Spark pounced into the air, carrying them both. Aber clutched Elenna's waist, looking terrified, while Elenna gripped Spark with her knees and shot arrow after arrow at the Beast. Each one fizzled to ashes on impact. While Flaymar staggered to regain her balance, Tom leapt onto Tempest and kicked his flanks. The stallion took

off, climbing steeply. Flaymar roared,
and Tom watched in horror as a whip
of fire unfurled from her hand. With
a flick of her wrist, it licked into the
sky and lashed itself around one of
Tempest's trailing legs. The stallion
whinnied in pain, but yanked free.

They surged out of reach.

"This isn't over!" Tom called back.

Flaymar grinned, her chest heaving. "I look forward to facing you again soon," she hissed.

Aber's face was black with smears of ash. The boy remained speechless as they flew back towards the town, but as they reached the edge of the lava lake, he managed to open his mouth. "Thank you," he said. "I never thought I'd get away."

"We've faced Beasts before," said Tom. "This one's no different."

Despite his confident words, inside he felt turmoil. How could he hope to defeat Flaymar? There wasn't enough water nearby to douse her body, and his sword seemed useless. To triumph over the other Evil Beasts of Henkrall, he'd had to get to their hearts, but

he couldn't possibly reach Flaymar's
– she was just too hot. Even now the
hairs on his arms were singed and his
tunic was marked with scorched holes
and tears.

They swooped over Herrinfell
towards the central square. "Let's be
prepared for a frosty welcome," Tom
said to Elenna. "After we've dropped
Aber off, we might need to leave in
a hurry."

Sure enough, as soon as their
animals landed on the cobbles,
townsfolk came running with their
weapons from two alleyways.

"I warned you!" shouted Prentas,
brandishing his spear.

Aber slipped out of the saddle,
standing in front of Tempest and Spark
with his arms raised. "Wait!" he said.

Another man lowered his sword

a fraction. "Aber?" he said. "Is that you?"

Prentas growled angrily. "Out of the way, boy."

"Stop!" said Aber. "They're our friends."

Prentas frowned. "What are you talking about?"

"These people rescued me," said Aber.

"Summon Jaffrey – quickly!" cried one of the women. Another man hurried off, and Prentas finally let his spear-point drop. His face was red, and he looked at the ground.

"It looks as though I judged you flightless folk too readily," he said.

"I don't blame you," Tom said. "Kensa has poisoned this kingdom with her evil."

Jaffrey arrived, leaning on a stick,

with Nema following on his heels.
"My boy!" he said. "You're safe!"

Aber ran into his grandfather's
embrace. "Thank you, thank you,"
Jaffrey said to Tom, with tears trailing
down his cheeks.

Nema stood in front on his friend
and looked towards his feet. "I'm sorry
I left you," he said. "I couldn't think
what else…"

"It's all right," said Aber to his friend.
"I'm just glad to be home." He smiled.

"In future, we can play tag in the town instead."

"Soon the town won't be safe either," Tom said. "Flaymar will cross the lava lake." He felt a stab of guilt – he knew that the Beast would stop at nothing to track him down. Had he put these people's lives in danger?

Prentas pointed up at the huge statue. "The Great Protector will scare off this Beast."

"The Protector's nothing but an over-sized scarecrow," replied a woman.

"I don't understand," said Elenna. "What does the writing up there mean?"

Jaffrey stared at the massive stone figure. "No one knows when it was erected," he said. "The myth is that a special hero can awaken it. Each person of the town has tried placing their palm on the plaque, but the giant has never moved."

"Maybe Tom should try," said Elenna.

This brought muttering from the townsfolk, and the woman called Olwyn jeered.

"We haven't got time for fairy tales," she said. "Aber's right – let's gather our valuables and flee with our lives."

Prentas shook his head. "There's something special about this flightless boy. Let him try."

"You have to prick your palm first," said Nema.

Elenna drew an arrow, and Tom understood. He held out his hand. He managed not to wince as Elenna nicked it with the tip of a shaft. Beads of blood trailed across his skin.

"He can't even get up there!" said Olwyn.

Prentas stepped forward. "Allow me."

Tom handed his sword and shield to Elenna, then let the man lift him beneath the armpits. They rose steadily up the front of the statue. Soon they were level with the marble plaque and the indented hand print.

Tom reached out and placed his bloody palm on the stone.

CHAPTER SEVEN

TIME OF NEED

Nothing happened.

"I told you so!" shouted Olwyn. "Fairy tales!"

"You need to believe in yourself," whispered Prentas.

Tom closed his eyes. He tried to block out the mutterings of the crowd below, and the soft beat of Prentas's wings as they hovered. He felt the strength of the golden breastplate swell in his heart. He and Elenna had faced so many Quests together – this couldn't be his last.

CRACK!

The spectators drew a collective gasp. Tom opened his eyes and saw the marble plaque had a narrow split down the centre. The two halves tumbled free and plummeted in the square below with a crash. The crowd leapt back and Tom was glad to see no one was hurt.

Beneath where the marble had been was a door leading into a hollow at the heart of the statue.

"I've never seen anything like it!" said Elenna, flying not far behind on Spark.

Tom barely heard her. He was staring inside at the strangest suit of armour he had ever laid eyes on. It

was made of bands of wicker, shaped
into a seated human form, just like
the statue itself.

A boy's form… Tom thought.

"Go to it," urged Elenna.

Prentas placed Tom inside the statue
where the plaque had been, and
backed away, his eyes wide. "It's like
it was meant to be…" he mumbled.

The two sections of the wooden
suit, a back and front, were fastened
with leather straps on one side.

"You need to wear it," said Elenna.

Tom wasn't sure how she knew that, but it felt like the right thing. He unfastened the clasps, stepped inside, and retied them. For a moment, he felt a rush of panic at being trapped, but it became a surge of power. Even though he was tiny compared with the enormous statue, he suddenly felt in control.

He slowly raised one arm. With a tremendous grinding sound, the Protector's stone arm lifted from his side, showering flakes of stone and moss onto the crowd below.

Tom's heart was thumping. *I did that!*

He raised his other arm and the statue's limb lifted too, stone grinding and columns of dust falling to the ground. It would have taken a hundred men, with horses and strong ropes, to lift the stone, but Tom was moving it as easily as his own limb!

Taking a deep breath, Tom straightened his legs. The Protector creaked upright from its sitting position, towering even higher than before over the square. Peering down from the statue's chest, Tom could see the amazed, upturned faces of the townsfolk.

"It's true!" Jaffrey cried.

"The Protector walks!" called Prentas.

Tempest whinnied and stamped his hooves. Tom waved down in the wicker suit and the Protector waved his table-sized hand in perfect time.

Elenna bobbed in front of him on Spark, grinning from ear to ear. "Are you ready to face Kensa's Beast?"

Tom flexed the giant fingers, feeling the crushing power of the Protector's grip. He shadow-boxed, pummelling the air with fists of stone. The statue responded in perfect time with his movements. "I'm ready!" he said.

He took a small step, lost his balance and staggered. The townsfolk scattered with frightened shouts, but Tom managed to steady himself. When he looked down he saw his foot had crunched through a cart laden with straw. "Sorry!" he called down.

This could take some getting used to!

But the next step was easier, and the next. Tempest flew to his side, whinnying.

"You can stay out of harm's way, this time," said Tom.

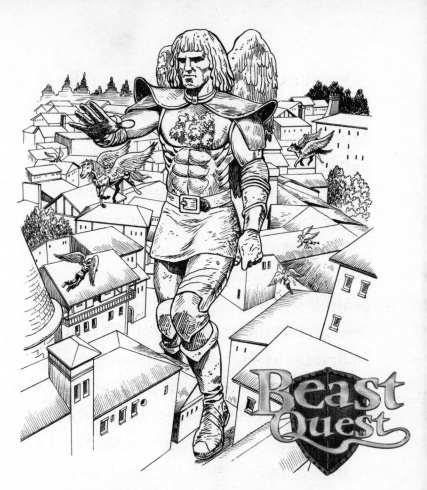

He picked his way between the
houses, placing his huge feet with
care. It reminded him of growing up
back in Errinel, taking care not to step
on trails of ants in his Uncle Henry's
yard.

When they reached the edge of the town, he took longer strides. Looking back, he saw his footprints in the earth. *I'm as big as a Beast!*

If Flaymar reaches this town, she'll leave more than footprints, he thought. *I can't let these people down.*

He broke into a run, feeling the ground shudder beneath his feet. The wicker suit shook his bones with each step, as the wind whipped past. Elenna flew full speed at his side.

The lava lake drew closer, with the dark smudge of geyser island squatted in the centre.

"How are you going to cross?" shouted his friend.

Tom heard her, but didn't slow. He called on the power of the golden leg armour, running faster and pumping his arms at his side.

"Wait!" shouted Elenna.

Tom could feel the giant's power – he knew he could make it. A few paces from the shoreline, he pushed off from the ground, sailing high over the bubbling lava. With a jarring thud he landed on the other side, crushing the charred vegetation beneath his feet.

He turned and saw Elenna flying across the lava, her face a mixture of amazement and relief. "You're just showing off now!" she called.

Tom grinned, then stared out across the island. Flaymar was waiting out there, somewhere. It was time to call her out.

Tom folded the Protector's stone arms across his chest, and shouted as loudly as he could.

"Are you ready to fight someone your own size, Kensa?"

CHAPTER EIGHT

STONE VERSUS FIRE

Flaymar's red and black form rose a hundred paces away, swelling from a crevasse in the ground. Smoke wreathed around her body, and flames spat from her limbs. Her red eyes narrowed. "What's this, Tom?" she asked.

"It's called levelling the odds," he replied.

Flaymar snarled and ran at him, whipping across the black rocks. Her cloak of fire scorched the ground in her wake. Tom stood firm, despite his brain telling him to run. He knew he had to trust in the strength of the Protector. *I might not be able to use my sword*, he thought, *but I've got other skills now*. Flaymar closed and reached for him with a fiery claw, but Tom kicked out. His stone foot caught

Flaymar in the midriff and sent
her flying. She landed on her back,
gasping with hissing breaths.

Tom advanced on the fallen Beast,
but she melted into a pool of lava and
flowed across the ground between
the Protector's legs. Tom felt the heat
as she rose on the other side. He'd
only half turned when two fiery arms
reached around him, pinning his own
arms to his side. Tom gritted his teeth
and struggled to free himself, but
Flaymar was too strong.

A rasping voice sounded in his ear.
"This lump of stone is no match for
my Beast!"

Smoke began to fill the Protector's
chest cavity, stinging Tom's eyes and
making him choke. It was hot too,
like a fire building all the time.

"Which would you prefer?" said

Flaymar. "Suffocation, or burning to death?"

Tom strained, but still he was trapped. *This stone is going to be my tomb!*

"He'd prefer to live!" shouted Elenna.

Tom saw his friend rise up through the smoke on Spark. In her hands was her bow, an arrow on the taut string. The shaft streaked past, and must have hit the Beast's shoulder, because Flaymar screamed and loosened her grip. Tom freed an arm and used both his hands to grip the Beast's shoulder, then bent his knees and threw Flaymar over his hip. The Scorched Blaze crashed to the ground in a shower of sparks and ash. Tom lifted his foot to stamp, but by the time it thumped into the ground, the Beast had done her disappearing act once more, melting into a geyser hole.

"Thanks," said Tom, to his friend. "Stay airborne. Flaymar might appear anywhere, and she'll be angrier than ever now."

Elenna pulled on Spark's fur and they climbed higher. "I'll keep a look out," she said. "Be careful."

Tom scanned the island, stepping over the rocks and through sickly green puddles. Geysers shot up like fountains, some mere bubbles, others fierce and thundering and tall as trees. Sprays of warm water, light as mist, settled on Tom's skin. He was beginning to see a weakness in the Great Protector. Strong as it was, turning around was slow. Tom couldn't shake the feeling there was something behind him, and that Flaymar would be able to spring up and pinion him in her arms once more.

I can trust Elenna to warn me, Tom reassured himself.

He stalked through the geysers in search of his prey. He needed to keep Flaymar still long enough to get to her heart – that was the key

to defeating the Beasts of Henkrall.
A sudden worry hit Tom. What if
Kensa had already directed Flaymar
back to the mainland to get the
Lightning Staff? She might already
be cutting a fiery swathe through
Herrinfell. He glanced towards the
town, using the power of the golden
helmet. He saw no smoke, no fire.

No, thought Tom, *Kensa will want to
deal with me first. That's what she said.*

"To your left!" Elenna called.

Tom turned and saw a geyser
shooting up thirty paces away, but it
wasn't water. It was fire! Instead of
cascading to the ground the flames
whipped into the shape of the
Beast. Flaymar seemed to burn even
brighter than before, white hot at her
edges and the tops of her limbs. Her
tangled red hair hung over her face.

"Come and get me!" said Tom, clenching his stone fists.

"Oh, I will!" hissed Flaymar.

She reached out a hand and in a single movement her fiery whip unfurled and lashed itself around the Protector's ankle. As Flaymar tugged sharply, Tom felt the giant's feet go

from under him. His world tipped as the statue toppled. The Protector landed with a bone-shaking crunch, snapping the clasps on the wicker suit and tossing Tom clear of the Protector's chest cavity. He landed with a cry and a painful thump, all the breath driven from his lungs.

When Tom managed to sit up, dizzy and bruised, he saw the Great Protector lying a few feet away on its side, lifeless and sprawled.

"Not so brave without your big friend, are you?" said Flaymar.

The Beast flicked her whip in the air with a crack.

The Scorching Blaze was coming for her revenge.

CHAPTER NINE

A FIERY DEATH

Tom reached for his sword, but realised too late it wasn't there.

I gave it to Elenna for safe keeping!

As Flaymar approached, he saw he couldn't reach the Protector. Any closer and she could simply smother him in flame. Just one swipe of Flaymar's whip would be enough to cut him in two.

But perhaps there was a way to stall

her. Tom saw a geyser hole to
his right and ran towards it.

"There's no escape," said Flaymar.

Tom tripped and fell headlong to
the ground. By the time he turned,
scrambling up, Flaymar was closing
in. She raised her whip. "You're mine
now!"

The geyser exploded between them,
showering them both with water.
Tom heard Flaymar's body sizzle,
releasing a vast cloud of steam. It
provided enough cover for Tom to
slip away, dashing towards the fallen
statue. By the time Flaymar had
worked out what was happening, he
was climbing inside the statue and
back into the battered wicker suit.

"No!" bellowed the Beast, dashing
towards him.

Tom's fingers scrambled to refasten

the leather clasps in quick, tight
knots, and he felt the old pulse of
power through his limbs. With one
fist balancing him on the ground,
the Protector leapt to his feet. At
the same time, Flaymar thrust out a
hand, trying to snatch at Tom inside
the statue. Tom blocked the hand
with a stone arm, then reached with
the Protector's other hand, plunging it
into the Beast's fiery chest. The giant's

fingers closed over something hard.

Flaymar's heart!

The Beast roared with fury, straining against Tom's blocking arm, trying to reach him with her white-hot fingers. Baking heat filled the wicker suit, making each breath a scorching agony. Tom squeezed the Beast's black heart in the Protector's fist, feeling it beating with pure evil.

"You're going to give up first!" he shouted.

Fire licked from Flaymar's eye-sockets and the jagged black slash of her mouth. Tom felt as if he was cooking on a stone oven. Fire seared his skin. Still he squeezed, blinking through palls of smoke. It took all his strength to stop the deadly snaking fingers from touching him.

"Don't give in, Tom!" Elenna cried.

His friend's voice gave him a surge of power. Tom squeezed with the wicker gauntlet and felt the heart firmly in the Protector's stone fist. He saw the white heat of Flaymar's limbs dim slightly. *I'm winning the battle!* He channelled all his strength to his hand, crushing with his fingers. The burning embers of the Beast's body began to melt. She was trying to escape, but while he held her life-force, she couldn't get away.

With a final jerk of his hand, Tom yanked Flaymar's black heart towards him.

Flaymar's eyes widened with shock. The flames blazing in their sockets extinguished as quickly as a blown out candle. Tom staggered backwards, the heart like a hot coal gripped in his hand.

"Look out!" Elenna cried.

Tom didn't understand until he saw the Protector's feet splashing into the lava. He'd stumbled off the island! Panic flooded Tom's veins, as he struggled to right himself, throwing up huge waves of molten lava. If he tripped over, he'd die in an instant. The Protector stumbled further out into the boiling mass, but Tom managed to stay upright. He held the heart up, as far from the lava as possible.

On the island, Flaymar shrieked, both hands clutching the space where her heart had been. Elenna flew over the ailing Beast, ready with an arrow for any surprises. But Tom could see this was the end. Flaymar's body dimmed to red, then orange as it shrank.

"This isn't over!" shrieked Kensa's voice. "This is not the end!"

With a final moan, she collapsing in

on herself like spent coals shifting in the hearth. The Scorching Blaze was defeated – nothing more than a pile of cooling boulders.

Tom tried to step back towards the shore, but his feet didn't budge. He strained, but they seemed to be stuck to the lake bed, as if buried in thick mud. He realised in horror that the stone of the statue's legs was crumbling.

I'm sinking into the lake!

He tried to unfasten the clasps on the wicker armour, but the knot was too tight. He couldn't reach his sword either because it was trapped against the inside of the suit.

"Help!" he called. "I'm stuck!"

Smoke billowed up from the spluttering lava, which was climbing quickly over the Protector's knees.

Elenna swooped down towards him on Spark, despite the choking smoke. She flew close to the chest opening and leapt off her animal, landing inside the cavity.

"I can't undo the knots," said Tom.

Elenna drew Tom's sword and sliced across the leather. Tom clambered out, then fell against Elenna as the Protector titled dangerously to one

side. The lava sloshed around its waist.

"It's melting," Tom said. "Where's Spark?"

"The smoke's too thick to see!" Elenna said, then broke off into a fit of coughing.

"We'll have to get to safety," said Tom. "Can you climb?"

He saw Elenna nod, her eyes streaming, as they scrambled out of the cavity and onto the Protector's vast chest. There were few handholds on the rough stone, but they managed to heave themselves higher, up the statue's shoulder. The Protector's arm was still reaching into the sky, clutching the Beast's heart.

The Protector began to shudder and wobble. It wouldn't be long before it toppled.

Spark had flown back to the island and was howling mournfully, flapping his wings with panic.

"It's too hot for him!" Elenna said.

We're on our own, thought Tom. *Elenna came here to rescue me, and now we're both going to die!*

CHAPTER TEN

BATTLE WON, WAR TO COME

The mighty statue creaked and sank lower into the lake. Tom imagined the stone beneath being eaten away by the lava. Without a flying steed, or a bridge of some sort, we're lost.

"That's it!" he said aloud. "A bridge! Follow me."

Tom hopped across the Protector's shoulder and onto the statue's outstretched arm. He began to shimmy along its length, as if he was climbing a tree branch back in Errinel.

"Oh, I get it!" Elenna said.

They both made their way up the arm and slowly their weight began to make it lean. The statue was tipping towards the shore. But would the arm be long enough?

"Faster!" called Tom, as the statue leaned further. Any moment, its own weight would topple it completely. He and Elenna scrambled desperately past the Protector's elbow and along his forearm.

The statue tipped suddenly. The lava rushed up to greet them. Tom seized Elenna's arm and hauled her the last few paces, leaping from the wrist of the Protector onto dry land.

A wave of lava broke over the bank, almost lapping their feet.

"We made it!" said Elenna. Spark the wolf rushed over and nuzzled her hand.

"The Great Protector didn't let us down," Tom replied. He watched sadly as the rest of the statue's body sank beneath the lava, the features of its noble face melting to become one with the spluttering molten rock. Only a single hand remained, fingers curled upwards, resting on the lake's edge.

"It fulfilled its mission," said Elenna.

"The town has been saved from a terrible fate."

Tom reached into the cupped hand and drew out Ferno's scale. As with each of the previous Quests, the heart had turned back into one of the Good Beast's magical tokens.

"I thought we might lose this," he said.

Elenna unhooked his shield from her back, and held it out so Tom could slot the scale into its rightful place.

A whinny made Tom look up. Tempest was circling.

"Looks like he came anyway," said Elenna. "That's good, because I don't think Spark fancied carrying us both."

Tom laughed as Tempest landed, glad to have his shield on his arm once more. "Let's head back to town."

"Our descendants will not believe what happened this day," said Jaffrey, speaking to the gathered townsfolk. He stood on the plinth where once the huge statue had sat. "Just as we puzzled over the Great Protector's origins, in the future they will speak of his rising as legend."

Tom stood beside Elenna and their animals at the front of the crowd.

"Even I can't believe it," Nema whispered, "and I watched it with my own eyes!"

"We have to thank two very special strangers," said Jaffrey. "They came from a foreign kingdom, but today they proved themselves friends of Henkrall. Place your hands together for Tom and—"

A bright flash of light from the

workshop made everyone gasp and cower. A few roof-tiles slipped off and smashed on the ground. Tom and Elenna broke away from the others and approached. Smoke trailed from cracks in the walls. "Who's there?" he called.

The doors at one end burst open, and a familiar hunchbacked figure darted out. He looked around shiftily.

"Igor!" Elenna cried.

Kensa's minion grinned, revealing toothless gums. "Greetings,

Avantians," he said. "Quite a fight you had over on Geyser Island. You were lucky."

Tom drew his sword. "What were you doing in there?" he asked.

With a snort, Igor's hog bundled out of the barn too. Igor heaved himself onto the animal's back. "Obeying my orders," he said, taking off.

"Flaymar's defeated!" Elenna yelled. "Tell Kensa her plan won't succeed."

Igor hovered above them. "Flaymar was nothing," he said. "Just a distraction. Kensa has the real prize!"

Prentas rose over the square. "Come on! After him!"

"Don't bother," said Jaffrey, his face clouded with worry. He was climbing down a ladder from the plinth. "If I'm right, it's too late."

"What do you mean?" asked Tom.

Jaffrey pointed to the open doors of the warehouse. "Look inside."

As Prentas landed, Tom rushed into the dark workshop and almost fell to his knees in shock. It was empty.

The staff had vanished.

"I'm such a fool!" said Jaffrey. "I should have known Kensa would use magic to steal the staff when it was ready."

Tom walked back into the daylight, stunned. "Defeating Flaymar was for nothing. Now Kensa will be able to transport a Beast to Avantia."

"Wait," said Elenna to Jaffrey. "Didn't you say before the staff was almost finished? Maybe Kensa won't be able to use it."

Jaffrey nodded weakly. "The staff itself is complete, but it will need a special jewel set into its head. That's what focuses the power of the lightning."

"And where are these jewels?" asked Tom.

"They're mined in the north," said Jaffrey. "For all I know, Kensa might already have one. All she needs then is a fork of lightning."

Tom felt a chill wind across his skin. He looked up, and saw to the east a black shadow across the horizon. Clouds were gathering in the sky, just like the ones in his heart. Just one flash of lightning and it could be the end.

We've got to defeat two more Beasts before that storm hits, he thought. *If Kensa gets even one of her creations to Avantia, it might be too late.*

He turned to Elenna. "Bad weather is coming," he warned her. "Our Quest just became even more deadly."

Join Tom on the next stage
of the Beast Quest when he meets

SERPIO
THE SLITHERING
SHADOW

Win an exclusive
Beast Quest T-shirt and goody bag!

Tom has battled many fearsome Beasts and we want to know
which one is your favourite! Send us a drawing or painting of
your favourite Beast and tell us in 30 words why you think
it's the best.

Each month we will select **three** winners to receive
a Beast Quest T-shirt and goody bag!

Send your entry on a postcard to
BEAST QUEST COMPETITION
Orchard Books, 338 Euston Road, London NW1 3BH.

Australian readers should email:
childrens.books@hachette.com.au

New Zealand readers should write to:
Beast Quest Competition, PO Box 3255, Shortland St,
Auckland 1140, NZ or email: childrensbooks@hachette.co.nz

**Don't forget to include your name and address.
Only one entry per child.**

Good luck!

All books priced at £4.99.
Special bumper editions priced at £5.99.

Orchard Books are available from all good bookshops, or can be ordered from our website: www.orchardbooks.co.uk, or telephone 01235 827702, or fax 01235 8227703.

Beast Quest ®

Series 11: THE NEW AGE
COLLECT THEM ALL!

A new land, a deadly enemy and six new Beasts
await Tom on his next adventure!

978 1 40831 841 6

978 1 40831 842 3

978 1 40831 843 0

978 1 40831 844 7

978 1 40831 845 4

978 1 40831 846 1

Meet six terrifying new Beasts!

Solak, Scourge of the Sea
Kajin the Beast Catcher
Issrilla the Creeping Menace
Vigrash the Clawed Eagle
Mirka the Ice Horse
Kama the Faceless Beast

Watch out for the next
Special Bumper
Edition

SPECIAL
BUMPER
EDITION!

OUT NOVEMBER 2012!

MEET A NEW HERO OF AVANTIA

ISBN: 978 1 40831 868 3

Dark magic has been unleashed!

Evil boy-Wizard Maximus is using the stolen golden gauntlet to wreak havoc on Avantia. A new hero must stand up to him, and battle the Beasts!

Join Tom on his Beast Quests
and take part in a terrifying adventure
where YOU call the shots!

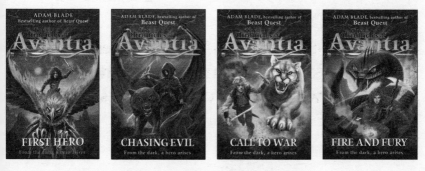

Read on for an exclusive extract of
CEPHALOX THE CYBER SQUID!

The Merryn's Touch

The water was up to Max's knees and still rising. Soon it would reach his waist. Then his chest. Then his face.

I'm going to die down here, he thought.

He hammered on the dome with all his strength, but the plexiglass held firm.

Then he saw something pale looming through the dark water outside the submersible. A long, silvery spike. It must be the squid-creature, with one of its weird robotic attachments. Any second now it would smash the glass and finish him off...

———

There was a crash. The sub rocked. The silver spike thrust through the broken plexiglass. More water surged in. Then the spike withdrew and the water poured in faster. Max forced his way against the torrent to the opening. If he could just squeeze through the gap...

The pressure pushed him back. He took one last deep breath, and then the water was

over his head.

He clamped his mouth shut. He struggled forwards, feeling the pressure in his lungs build.

Something gripped his arms, but it wasn't the squid's tentacle – it was a pair of hands, pulling him through the hole. The broken plexiglass scraped his sides – and then he was through.

The monster was nowhere to be seen. In the dim underwater light, he made out the face of his rescuer. It was the Merryn girl, and next to her was a large silver swordfish.

She smiled at him.

Max couldn't smile back. He'd been saved from a metal coffin, only to swap it for a watery one. The pressure of the ocean squeezed him on every side. His lungs felt as though they were bursting.

He thrashed his limbs, rising upwards.

He looked to where he thought the surface was, but saw nothing, only endless water. His cheeks puffed with the effort to hold in air. He let some of it out slowly, but it only made him want to breathe in more.

He knew he had no chance. He was too deep, he'd never make it to the surface. Soon he'd no longer be able to hold his breath. The water would swirl into his lungs and he'd die here, at the bottom of the sea. *Just like my mother*, he thought.

The Merryn girl rose up beside him, reached out and put her hands on his neck. Warmth seemed to flow from her fingers. Then the warmth turned to pain. What was happening? It got worse and worse, until he felt as if his throat was being ripped open. Was she trying to kill him?

He struggled in panic, trying to push her off. His mouth opened and water rushed in.

That was it. He was going to die.

Then he realised something – the water was cool and sweet. He sucked it down into his lungs. Nothing had ever tasted so good.

He was breathing underwater!

He put his hands to his neck and found two soft, gill-like openings where the Merryn

girl had touched him. His eyes widened in astonishment.

The girl smiled.

There was something else strange. Max found he could see more clearly. The water seemed lighter and thinner. He made out the shapes of underwater plants, rock formations and shoals of fish in the distance, which had been invisible before. And he didn't feel as if the ocean was crushing him any more.

Is this what it's like to be a Merryn? he wondered.

"I'm Lia," said the girl. "And this is Spike." She patted the swordfish on the back and it nuzzled against her.

"Hi, I'm Max." He clapped his hand to his mouth in shock. He was speaking the same strange language of sighs and whistles he'd heard the girl use when he first met her –

but now it made sense, as if he was born to speak it.

"What have you done to me?"

"Saved your life," said Lia. "You're welcome, by the way."

"Oh – don't think I'm not grateful – I am. But – you've turned me into a Merryn?"

The girl laughed. "Not exactly – but I've given you some Merryn powers. You can breath underwater, speak our language, and your senses are much stronger. Come on – we need to get away from here. The Cybersquid may come back."

In one graceful movement she slipped onto Spike's back. Max clambered on behind her.

"Hold tight," Lia said. "Spike – let's go!"

Max put his arms around the Merryn's waist. He was jerked backwards as the swordfish shot off through the water, but he managed to hold on.

———

They raced above underwater forests of gently waving fronds, and hills and valleys of rock. Max saw giant crabs scuttling over the seabed. Undersea creatures loomed up – jellyfish, an octopus, a school of dolphins – but Spike nimbly swerved round them.

"Where are we going?" Max asked.

"You'll see," Lia said over her shoulder.

"I need to find my dad," Max said. The crazy things that had happened in the last few moments had driven his father from his mind. Now it all came flooding back. Was his dad gone for good? "We have to do something! That monster's got my dad – and my dogbot too!"

"It's not the squid who wants your father. It's the Professor who's *controlling* the squid. I tried to warn you back at the city – but you wouldn't listen."

"I didn't understand you then!"

———

"You Breathers don't try to understand – that's your whole problem!"

"I'm trying now. What is that monster? And who is the Professor?"

"I'll explain everything when we arrive."

"Arrive where?"

The seabed suddenly fell away. A steep valley sloped down, leading way, way deeper than the ocean ridge Aquora was built on. The swordfish dived. The water grew darker.

Far below, Max saw a faint yellow glimmer. As he watched it grew bigger and brighter, until it became a vast undersea city of golden-glinting rock rushing up towards them. There were towers, spires, domes, bridges, courtyards, squares, gardens. A city as big as Aquora, and far more beautiful, at the bottom of the sea.

Max gasped in amazement. The water was dark, but the city emitted a glow of its own

– a warm phosphorescent light that spilled
from the many windows. The rock sparkled.
Orange, pink and scarlet corals and seashells
decorated the walls in intricate patterns.

"This is – amazing!" he said.

Lia turned round and smiled at him. "It's our home," she said. "Sumara!"

———

IF YOU LIKE BEAST QUEST, YOU'LL LOVE ADAM BLADE'S NEW SERIES